FARMER GLOOMY'S NEW HYBRID

ECW PRESS

For Lynn,
Poddily

Love,
Sfh

12 oct 99

CANADIAN CATALOGUING IN PUBLICATION DATA

Ross, Stuart, 1959–
Farmer Gloomy's new hybrid

Poems
ISBN 1-55022-394-1

I. Title.
PS8585.O841F37 1999   C811'.54   C99-931984-1
PR9199.3.R67F37 1999

Cover and text design by Tania Craan
Cover collage by Michael Richardson
Author photo by Paul Forsyth
Edited for the press by Michael Holmes
Layout by Mary Bowness
Printed by AGMV l'Imprimeur, Cap-Saint-Ignace, Québec

Distributed in Canada by General Distribution Services,
325 Humber Blvd., Etobicoke, Ontario M9W 7C3

Published by ECW PRESS
2120 Queen Street East, Suite 200,
Toronto, Ontario, M4E 1E2
www.ecw.ca/press

The publication of *Farmer Gloomy's New Hybrid* has been generously
supported by The Canada Council, the Ontario Arts Council, and
the Government of Canada through the Book Publishing
Industry Development Program.

ACKNOWLEDGEMENTS

Some of these poems have appeared, often in earlier versions, in the magazines *Alien Cookbook, Bomb Threat Checklist, CB: A Poetry Magazine, Geist, Mental Radio, Perpetual Motion Machine, Torque, WHAT!*, and *Who Torched Rancho Diablo?*; in the anthologies *Carnival: A Scream in High Park Reader* (Insomniac Press), *Hard Times: A New Fiction Anthology* (The Mercury Press), *The Instant Anthology 1998* (Toronto Small Press Group), *Snapshots: The New Canadian Fiction* (Black Moss Press), and *The WHIPlash 2 Reader* (above/ground press); as the chapbooks *Cigarettes* (Proper Tales Press), *In This World* (Berkeley Horse), *Say Fway Luh Looz* (Proper Tales Press), and *Sitting by the Judas Hole* (Proper Tales Press); and as leaflets and broadsides published by Proper Tales Press, 1cent, and above/ground press. Thanks go directly to the editors of these publications, and, as always, to the organizers of readings where I gave these pieces workouts.

"Plaintive Poultry" was written under a title suggested by Kevin Connolly; "Passed Over" was written under a title inspired by a song by Son Volt; "Landscape" was written between the lines of the Larry Fagin poem of the same title. "Carcass Status" is for Sarah Dearing; "Say Fway Luh Looz" is for *compañero* Joe Grengs.

Huge thanks and a few pints to Kevin Connolly for knowing my work so well and calling me on my furtive attempts at fraud; thanks also to ECW editor Michael Holmes for his support and suggestions, to Paul Dutton for his wise nitpicks on a few poems, to Alana Wilcox for an astute proofread, and especially to Judy MacDonald for her excellent comments on an earlier version of this manuscript. Encouragement also came from Sydney Ross, Sean and Neil Wilson, Michael Dennis, and others I'm too tired and unshaven to remember right now.

I'm grateful for the support of the citizens of Ontario through the Ontario Arts Council, and the citizens of Toronto through the Toronto Arts Council.

SELECTED OTHER BOOKS BY THE AUTHOR

POETRY

The Inspiration Cha-Cha (ECW Press, 1996)

Dusty Hats Vanish (Proper Tales Press, 1994)

Little Black Train (Proper Tales Press, 1993)

Ladies & Gentlemen, Mr. Ron Padgett (Proper Tales Press, 1989)

Paralysis Beach (Pink Dog Press, 1988)

He Counted His Fingers, He Counted His Toes
(Proper Tales Press, 1978)

FICTION

The Results of the Autopsy: 13 Little Love Stories
(Proper Tales Press, 1999)

Mr. Joe (Proper Tales Press, 1998)

Language Lessons with Simon and Marie!
(as Estuardo Rossini; Proper Tales Press, 1998)

Henry Kafka and Other Stories (The Mercury Press, 1997)

The Mud Game (with Gary Barwin; The Mercury Press, 1995)

The Pig Sleeps (with Mark Laba; Contra Mundo Press, 1993)

Mr. Style, That's Me (Proper Tales Press, 1991)

Guided Missiles (Proper Tales Press, 1990)

Captain Earmuff's Agenda (The Front Press, 1987)

Wooden Rooster (Proper Tales Press, 1986)

Father, the Cowboys Are Ready to Come Down from the Attic
(Proper Tales Press, 1982)

CONTENTS

HOW TO SUCCEED

"Brain, shake out thy water, dog-like."

RON PADGETT

TENGO FUEGO

AFTER THE EVENT,
BUT BEFORE THE THING THAT HAPPENED

I ran from the lightning. I ran from the legless duck. I ran from the collapsing building. I ran from the bad boy. I ran from the cob of corn. I ran from the incorrect professor. I ran from Walking After Midnight. I ran from the flailing midwife. I ran from the stench. I ran from the collapsing democracy. I ran from the happy dreidl. I ran from the moon's gaunt face. I ran from my sister's shadow. I ran from the porcelain antelope. I ran from the runaway station wagon. I ran from my sense of humour. I ran from a lump. I ran from alcohol and flashlights. I ran from peeling wallpaper. I ran from bondage. I ran from a Hardy Boys novel and left Chet Morton behind. I ran from television. I ran from Immanuel Kant. I ran from off-key troubadours. I ran from the axe. I ran from adolescence. I ran from the sneaky cartoon. I ran from cost-effectiveness. I ran from the limp squeezebox. I ran from chicken bones. I ran from fascist clip-art. I ran from the constant defender. I ran from the shadow of a cloud pursuing me across a desert whose sands spilled over every horizon.

THE SHOPPING MALL

At night a shopping mall
is cold and sad.
It flattens itself,
crawls across the
empty expanse of its parking lot,
squeezes under a gleaming archway
that says Shop And Be Happy.
Soon it is
inching along the road;
it has forgotten
its loneliness.
In the glare of the streetlamps,
the mall is indistinguishable
from the pavement.
The telephone wires
don't give it away;
they sway in the crisp air,
mutter amongst themselves.
The fire hydrants are silent,
and so are the mailboxes.
Stray dogs sniff at the creeping mall,
then bound off,
paws ripping lawns,
shrill yaps cracking
the thick clouds above.

Torrents of rain begin to fall
and the mall becomes frightened.
It crawls up to a house
and through an open window.
It is in a small room.
It recognizes the posters on the wall
from its record shop
and the books on the shelf
from its book shop
and the carpet from its
wholesale carpet outlet
and the dresser and desk and bed
from its furniture store
and the lamp on the desk
from its lighting store
and the boy in the bed
from its video arcade.
The shopping mall
creeps up onto the bed
and wraps itself around the boy's chin,
clinging tight to the smooth face.
In the morning, the boy's parents
are astonished when he comes to breakfast.
"You are not yet seven,
but you have a beard,"
says the father, and they
lock him in his room.

Pilgrims come from around the world

to see the bearded boy.

His eyes are wide.

He wants to shave.

He is blessed by the pope,

and by movie stars,

by hockey players

and famous models.

The steady stream of people

passing by his bed,

night and day,

becomes overwhelming.

The boy is cold and sad.

A policeman looks at a calendar –

the mall went missing

the day the bearded boy appeared!

He hauls the child out of bed

and drags him to the cruiser.

The boy is excited.

He asks the officer to turn on the siren.

He asks the officer to make the red lights flash.

They speed through sleeping streets,

then across an empty parking lot

surrounding a vast, dark chasm.

"I remember this place,"

says the boy,

"I know I've been here before."

The policeman places the child
in the centre of the emptiness
and takes a few steps back.
The boy tugs at his beard,
writhes and wrestles,
thrashes his arms and legs.
The beard is so tight
he can barely breathe.
He lies down exhausted
and falls asleep.
A car pulls into the lot,
and then another.
The officer begins directing traffic.
Soon the boy is teeming with shoppers.
"Where's the cinema?" they ask.
"Where's the Mexican restaurant?"
Shopping at the boy
is not as convenient,
but humans are clever
and patient.
They have weathered many changes.
They are strong.
They adapt.

TENGO FUEGO

I have fire, I have
a light, I got a
match, right here
in my shirt pocket, right –
Shit, it's gone,
my shirt is gone,
I groped my own breast.
Looking for a match
to light this cigarette
dangling from my lips
I groped *me*. Yee-ha.
Nobody noticed.
They went on sipping their
coffees, talking about Truffaut
and Derrida, about
elves and elks, about British
miners, about nice boys.
A girl with glasses, she looks
real smart, just looked in
my direction, yee-ha.
She's smoking, I run my fingers
through her tangled hair –
in my *dreams*, I do!
Yee-ha. I'm an eel,
a cigar, a banana,
a cannon. I'm tiny

and I climb up the side
of my coffee mug and tumble
in. Yikes! Someone help me!
I wave my little armitos
but no one sees me.
I have become a common housefly
drowning in my own coffee,
coffee that *I* paid for –
imagine that!
The girl with glasses is
getting up, she's putting on
her jacket, she's walking out
the door. I am helpless. My wings
are drenched.
I sink to the bottom
of the mug. I lie there
and try to buzz.
I remember my dog.
He will be sitting by his dish
waiting for food.
Waiting for me
to come and feed him.
But I've become a drowned fly
and I will not come home
to feed my dog.
Poor little
droopy-eyed thing.

NO PLACE LIKE HOME

I took the standard tour
of the Planet Without Oxygen
and fell in love
with a melancholy crustacean.
We built ourselves a little home
in a desert town
where we hoped to
pass what few years
remained to us.
I had a trunk
full of photo albums
and these we wept over
without even opening them.
An abrupt knock on the door
shook us from our resigned
decline. A long-lost son,
perhaps a telegram from the dead,
or a wife
presumed killed in battle.
A change. A
new tune. Sixty-four
tiny bipeds carrying us
through the streets,
the throngs cheering
and throwing gold pieces.

A smile without pain.
A sigh erupting and
splitting the earth.

BULLETIN

We interrupt this poem
for an important bulletin,
for a stunning medical breakthrough,
for a boxing match,
for a glass of 1934 Chardonnay,
for the discovery of life on other planets,
for little Jimmy's new leg brace,
for a derailed train, its passengers screaming,
for an appointment with your therapist,
for an empty bird's nest,
for a few tips on nostril depilation,
for an urgent meeting by world leaders,
for a cigarette, the last in the pack,
for a frayed electrical cord,
for a yodelling contest,
for anything,
for god's sake,
but the poem.

PENALTIES

I asked too many questions
and the ability to
walk through walls
was taken away from me.

The stick figures that had visited me
only in my dreams
began populating
my waking hours,
replacing first the strangers
who passed me on the sidewalk
and later my workmates
and family.
It got so I could
tell my mother from my father
only by the single line of hair
that curled up each side of her head.
This was not
what I considered
a healthy environment.

I appealed the decision
and they slapped more penalties
on me. Music all sounded
like scraping; the sky

was no longer visible;
books fell apart in my hands.

I applied for residency
in a parallel universe
and I was offered a hamburger.

I'll read a few lines
from the letter they sent:
"Citizen,
your aggression
harms only
yourself.
Also,
please note
that bingo nights
have been switched
to Thursdays."

I wish I'd known
they had bingo.

1993

Radio sizzling between stations
in the next apartment
Candle wax splattered across the table
Here: scrape the tears from your face with this
Kick off your shoes
Throw everything into the pot
while the fire's going
One of these days you open the window
& it smells like Managua
or wherever you dream of
Some boll weevils reading
Faulkner on the curb &
though the wind has called it a day
the tire in the tree keeps swinging
Yeah well
i'm lying on the floor
humming labour songs
& someone's coming
to fix something

NO LIFE LIKE IT

I travel to work
in a long metal tube
that hurtles through tunnels
beneath city streets.
It is a subway.
When I arrive at the office building,
which is a big rectangle stood on its end,
containing many little compartments
and clear things you can look through,
I have to climb a few steps,
which are regular floors, but jagged,
before I reach the door,
a piece of wood
thin as a cartoon character
squashed by a steamroller.
My desk is a decapitated zebra
with a very flat back and my chair
a tree stump with little wheels
and I sit in front of a heavy rectangular box
with a square box sitting on top. This
is my computer. I do things
on it. And at lunch hour I open my
brown paper bag – a cow's stomach! –
and I eat two square white tiles
with some orange tiles inside.

All around me in the office
are these tall cylindrical devices,
lumbering along on two thin sticks,
waving two other sticks
that protrude from their sides.
And stuck on top
is a sphere sprouting fine spaghetti.
They ask me questions and give me orders;
I become scared and drop things;
I cover my ears to stop their shrill bleating;
I watch the round thing with numbers
and pray that soon I can leave.

COFFEE BREAK

I don't speak English.

It is a bad language.

Give me an onion.

A MESSAGE TO THE POPULACE

My arms are wide

and welcoming.

Listen:

I found an egg under the hood of a stolen car.

There was writing on it:

POPO THE PIG

SAYS COME TO THE PORK ROAST.

I duly presented it to the authorities,

who rewarded me

with a kiss to the forehead.

I left the station,

something dragging on my shoe.

A piece of paper stuck there.

It said POPO THE PIG

SAYS COME TO THE PORK ROAST.

I ran to the arms of my father,

the hairy loopy arms of my papa.

"POPO THE PIG,"

I said breathlessly.

"What?" he urged, his thumbs

pressing tight against my throat.

"What of it?"

"POPO THE PIG

SAYS COME TO THE PORK ROAST."

My father loosened his grip

and gave me the keys
to the bowling ball.
He said: "The pig
is happy and diversion
vis-à-vis the barbecue.
Its smile a rainbow from ear to ear.
Now you are a leader.
The community is up in arms.
Present your snout
to the mobs. Establish
mildly a stranglehold
on their grief. We
are history. A slice
from Popo's flank
brings calm and
relentless good posture
to the milling populace."
I accepted the tall man's blessing
and here I am, before you.
Do you know about Popo?
Popo is the happy pig.
Reach deep into your chest
where you have so many hearts.
Give one of those
to each of me.

BUT, MISTER, THEY NO HAVE BOWLING BALLS
BEFORE CHRIST

This supermarket
is my favourite supermarket.

Children plant bombs on the pony ride.
Peacekeepers are blown into the frozen food section.
They begin to think they're niblets.

When the muzak stops,
the shoppers exchange lists.

The shelves are full of disgruntled products.
A box of crackers coughs in my face.
A bottle of soda mocks my beliefs.

I want to buy a bowling ball.
A woman tells me to take a number and wait my turn.

Farmer Gloomy introduces new hybrids.
They make the aisles wiggly.

The rice is so instant it is already eaten.

I replace my tongue with that of a cow.

I am voted fourth most popular shopper.

A rabbi faints in the checkout line.

I leave empty-handed.

GRAMMATICAL ERRORS

I

Dangling Modifier

Leaving the bar one night,
Li Po was waiting outside
to punch me out.

II

Dangling Preposition

It is my head
that my eyes
popped out of.

THE HAPPY

He didn't have a name, but even if he had, it wouldn't
have helped him crawl any faster.

A name wouldn't have stopped the bleeding at his
fingertips and palms, his knees, the pads of his toes.

A name – like Buck, or Charlie – wouldn't have
provided a pillow for his weary head.

If he were William, his throat would still feel like
sandpaper.

If he were Vladimir, Tomás, or Pierre, his eyes wouldn't
be any less gritty with dust.

But he was happy.

He couldn't sing, or find the energy to click his heels, but
he was happy.

He didn't need a name to be happy.

In fact, had his name been Happy, he wouldn't have been
any happier.

He had two legs, and sometimes he simply dragged them along.

He had two arms, and these he used to pull his increasingly light body.

What more did he need?

Oh, sure, a change of clothes – a fresh shirt, at least – would have been nice, but it wasn't a matter of life and death.

And, really – what was?

Only that he should continue breathing, his heart should pump blood, his hair should keep growing.

He looked at you and said, "I once ate a hamburger."

And he crawled on, happy.

THE ROOM

The room is bleak
and quiet
and in the bleak room
is a bleak room
that is very bleak.
And in the room
that is very bleak
there is a bleak
bleak room and
there it is very
very bleak and
around this bleak room
is a room
that's small and bare and
quiet and also bleak
and there is a bleak room there,
a room that is quiet
and bleak,
rather bleak,
and the door opens
onto the bleak room
and a man
with wide lapels
walks in.

SITTING BY THE JUDAS HOLE

SITTING BY THE JUDAS HOLE

They rip the door off its hinges,
dash it to the floor.
They say, Now you can leave.

I walk out onto the porch,
squint against the sun.
There's a man in a cap
at the edge of my lawn,
his arm rotates like a windmill,
faster and faster,
I hear it whistling.
I know him somehow
from many years back.
He yells,
"I'm not on your property,
I'm on the road!"

His jaw slides up and down
and I wonder, Is this guy
a puppet?
Or is he dubbed?
His words don't match
his mouth.

But forget the mouth,

the pinwheel arm is a blur,
a Ferris wheel out of control.
Children are screaming,
clutching each other in fear.

And then it is still. The arm
is still. But I can still
hear a whistling – not the
whistle of the arm. The arm
is still.
Something else appears.
It gets bigger and bigger.

"I'm not on your property,
I'm on the road!"
Yeah, but I saw his foot on the curb,
the curb's my property.

And they say, The curb belongs to the city.

But the curb's my property. My property
ends at the curb, but includes
the curb. The curb –

Something slams into
the bridge of my nose, I want
to vomit, I stumble back,

right back into my house, and
through tear-filled eyes I see a ball
rolling off the porch, a baseball.
It comes to a stop on my lawn.

The front of my shirt is bloodied.
I am aghast – I've just had it dry-cleaned.
I have the receipt to prove it.
Please replace my door.

* * *

I sit in a chair
facing the closed door.
My forehead leans beneath
the Judas hole.
I hear footsteps on my porch.
Sir Robert Falcon Scott.
I loved Sir Robert Falcon Scott.
John Dillinger.
I loved John Dillinger. He did not die.
Montgomery Clift.
I loved Montgomery Clift.
I loved his eyes,
the way they watered.
He did not die.
Sir Robert Falcon Scott
is very cold.
I shiver.
My ankles are bound
in plastic cord;
I cannot dance.
The cord snakes through
the legs of the chair,
down the hallway,
through the kitchen,
and into another hallway beyond,
to my telephone.
The cord is attached to the telephone.

If the telephone rings I'll scream.
The telephone is the monster
that carries her voice, carries all
their voices. I remember her voice.
Her voice is the sound of my heart
thudding to a stop,
falling flat on its face.
My heart is a cartoon.
It is projected on the wall.
It is a beached whale;
it wheezes in the sand.
I'd like you to meet my heart.

* * *

You shiver, your forehead
rattling against the door.
The faintest sound of scratching
reaches your ears.
And little plops, you think
you hear little plops,
the sound of lizards hitting the floor.
Above your head,
someone is peering in.
Isn't that the rustling of eyelashes?
Isn't that the twang
of legs stretching?
Something brushes against your foot
and you convulse. You jerk your feet
from the floor,
place them on a rung of the chair.
"Lizards," you say.
"Lizards."
If greenbeans had legs
and two beady eyes, and
if greenbeans could scurry
and flick their tongues,
then greenbeans would be lizards.
With lizards falling from the walls
and strangers peeping through the door,
you change your tune.
"Greenbeans," you say.

"Greenbeans."
After a few hours
you've become dogmatic –
that is to say,
you've become your own best friend.

* * *

This is certain:
somewhere someone
was once in love.
Murmurs curled through the thick smoke
of candles. Ankles were entwined.
In the dark sky, glimpses of a setting
sun were caught between mountains
of orange cloud. There was breath on a neck.
A hair on a pillow.

Now there is the roar
of the city, the squealing
of tires, the howling of dogs
fucking in busy intersections,
the slam of elevators at every floor,
the deafening rattle of streetcars
delivering corpses.

Step into a bakery.
Buy bread and eat it.
Tear it with your teeth.
Buy yourself a paper bag
and put something in it.
Then buy a newspaper and
throw it in the air.
See how it lands in the hands

of those who want it?

Rent a car.

Drive it into a ravine.

I hear a whisper follow me. I run
around a corner and catch my breath.

* * *

A piece of paper slides under
the door. It hits my toes.
I open my clenched-shut eyes.
Blobs of colour float around
my field of vision,
till finally I can
make out the writing on
the flyer. It says Chinese
Food, it says Tea Leaves Readings,
it says Half-Price Snowtires, it says
Hot Dogs All-Dressed. It says a
neighbourhood committee is being formed
to catch the second-floor rapist, it says
my Conservative member of parliament
is doing a cracker job, it says
recycling boxes will be distributed
to Every Fucking Household.

Each letter is cut
from a different source
and pasted down haphazardly.
It says We HavE YOuR chILd,
WE wANt yoUr MOneY,
wE Buy aLL yoUR cARRotS,
we Like YOUr haiRCUt.

I dangle one arm

like a worm on a hook
and pick up the paper.
I turn it over. I
read it. The blobs are
gone from my eyes, I can
read now. It says,
"I'm standing here
this side of the door.
I'm waiting for you.
I'm as bad as you remember.
Please open up. I love you."
The handwriting is familiar.
It belongs to everyone
I've ever known.
They took turns, one letter
each, an exquisite corpse,
a chain of fools, dominoes made
of razor blades.

It's good for a laugh. I
unfold the paper.
It is a note from my landlord.
I've missed my rent.
He wonders how many bodies I've
buried under the floorboards.
He is eager to excavate.
He will find nothing.

There is nothing to find.

I'm crazy with love
but I keep forgetting.

* * *

I would like to talk about death now.

Did you see the puddles in the grave?

Did you see the gravediggers nearby,

heads hanging, hands folded?

Did you see the shovels jammed in the dirt?

Did you see the pallbearers' faces?

Did you see the rust on the sides of the hearse?

Did you hear the rabbi's voice shake?

Did you hear the son's voice shake?

Did you hear the bus drive by while they lowered the coffin?

Did you see the ad on the side of the bus?

Did you read the ad?

Do you remember the product?

Will you buy some?

Will you buy *me* some?

* * *

They say:
The guests will begin arriving
in forty-five minutes. You've got
to remove your head from the door
and pull yourself together.

I say:
I didn't call this party.
There are lizards on my wall.

They say:
Have you prepared the hors d'oeuvres?
They'll expect little sandwiches,
bowls of nuts, glasses of wine,
vegetables and dip. They'll expect
a smile on your face. They'll expect
music. Music for dancing. Dance
music.

I say:
My body is a lead weight.
I cannot move. Lizards
crawl about my shoulders and neck.
I'm too tired even
to shudder in revulsion. I'm afraid
I'm unable
to entertain right now.

They say:

But can't you hear them?

They are preparing to leave,

buttoning their shirts,

knotting their ties,

rolling on their nylons,

clearing their throats,

climbing into their cars.

They have little pieces of tissue

stuck to their shaving cuts.

I say:

Hey! Somebody put something

in my cyanide!

* * *

My enemy has held his grudge for far too long.
The grudge is the size of a croquet ball,
and wet and yielding as clay.
He holds the grudge in his hands,
rotating it, staring into it.
Each day it becomes smaller and harder.
It becomes more precise.
It burns his hands
and he turns it more quickly.
He can see to the very centre
of the grudge in his hands,
he can see its heart,
the heart's teeth clenched.
When I pass my enemy in the street,
he tucks his grudge in his coat
and sneers. I am stoic. Calm.
His hatred singes my sideburns.
I say, "Hello," and the sky turns dark.
A gale builds and sweeps us into an alley.
We come to in each other's arms.
His hands go for my throat, mine for his.
We are hard. We make guttural noises.
He squeezes my soul up my throat
and out my mouth. It takes flight.
I hear it howl on this day dark like night.

* * *

You pull yourself up slowly
till your eye is at the hole.
You squawk. Your porch
is empty, there is no one
there. In the distance,
you see layers of snow
covering the tent of
Sir Robert Falcon Scott's
doomed expedition. Scott sits
inside with Bowers and Wilson,
while Oates's selfless footprints
fade now, trailing
from the tent
to windswept oblivion.
The tent is tidy, they did
the dishes before they died,
and Scott is clutching his
journal. You can almost
read it from here,
but you gotta really squint:
"It seems a pity, but
I do not think I can
write more . . ."
You blink
and it's all gone.
The street is dark,
the lights in every home

are off. Cranes reach from the sky
and pluck the roofs
from houses,
silent, silent,
hands begin to appear,
and heads, shoulders,
faces peering over the
tops of walls, men,
women and children crawling
up and out, down
the sides of their homes.
They are free. They crawl
across their lawns and
down the street, past
the 7-Elevens, the laundromat,
past the school and past
the offices.
There is an Arctic waiting,
an Antarctic, a jungle,
a river, there is a great
open field where they can
tilt back their heads
and scream.

* * *

LOOKING INTO MY ILLNESS

PASSED OVER

I was passed over
by the streams of broken-down cars
flowing off the edge of the cliff
I was passed over
by the tangled canopies of knotted branches
collapsing on the shoppers in aisle 7
I was passed over
by the 100 eager mothers
waving snapshots of their babies
by the quivering hungry ledger
of a weaving scrum of accountants
by umbrellas concealing hypodermics
and elbows firing hollow-tip bullets
passed over by smiling best-sellers
and growling milkmen
and weeping dentists
and by a horizonful of devious deathclouds
dressed as ticket-takers at a family fun fair
by giant lumbering banana people
drunken ex-models slumped over transistor radios
infant politicians in glittering heels
an expanse of frustrated pavement
a big bug
a very big bug with an armoured thorax
it's got long spindly legs

with hairs poking out
somebody will make a movie about it
it'll lurch through the dirt
and eat other bugs
it will endure heartbreak
and natural disaster
in the end it will triumph
that's some movie
everyone should see it

THE RING

But in the back of the bar on the
TV that boxer bites off that other
boxer's ear, then his other ear
and his nose. Soon he's eaten the
whole head and is gnawing along
the neck like it was barbecued
corn. "Usually I have my big meal
earlier in the day," he says to
the cameras, "so I can burn it
off before I sleep, but tonight,
I dunno, even with nowhere to
tuck my bib, I just got the craving.
I know I am not the best
role model and I urge the youth
of America to condemn my actions
and do what is right. Never eat
your opponent after lunch or as a
between-meals snack."

The glare of the lights
above the ring, reflecting
off a thousand sweaty
foreheads, refracting through the
curling hissing smoke of a
thousand wagging cigars,

disguises the flight of a moth
that rises from between the
shoulders of the headless boxer
and sails right through the TV
screen, into the bar, where it
alights on the bartender's
shoulder. The bartender does not
yet know his house is empty, his
lover is gone, a terse note
awaits his return,
after a walk through
the cold drizzle, under
flickering streetlamps, through
sidewalks teeming with headless
boxers, their gloved hands raised
in ecstasy.

VELVET CURTAINS

In the cinema, I sit in the front row,
and the flickering screen is so big,
Robert Mitchum's shadowed face so vast,
I gotta tilt my head way back.
A rope unravels, dangles
before my eyes. I grasp it
and am lifted, slowly, towards the ceiling.
I pass by Shelley Winters' glistening brow
and feel popcorn rain on me like kisses.
And when I reach the rafters and the lights,
look down upon the crowns of a hundred heads,
a woman with hair of seaweed takes my hand,
says, "Hey, it's good to have you back among the dead."
And she shows me how the velvet
curtains work, the mysterious
velvet curtain mechanism,
and we glide across the ceiling
like we're at Arthur Murray's.
"It's cloudy here," I murmur, because it is.

As she brushes the cloud from my hair,
I admit that once I drove a bus
and wore a moustache. I wandered through the forests
singing hymns. I slept in a barn
and counted sheep to sleep.

"Abide the children," she said,
"the gentle shivering omelettes." And I –
who once across the river leapt –
knelt, undid my laces, and exhaled.

YAKETY-YAK

Me, I
dive into
the wilting cardboard box
in storage at Dad's,
find a tangle of toys and
string and coins and
rolled-up paintings I painted
30 years ago, their edges
brittle, flaking. I remember
those canisters of rich powdered
paint: just add water and
three decades pass.
I ache
in the most maudlin
way, shuffle
into the kitchen, open
a can of niblets, eat 'em
cold. From the living room
I hear some coughing
above the sound of the TV.
It's a man
who is my father.

CARCASS STATUS

Inquiring discreetly about the carcass status
of the hunting jacket upon which fell
my eyes and heart, I was assured
through a cloud of velvet cigarette smoke
that no dead rabbits would turn up
in the lining. I did not wish, like,
to offend the proprietor (of the hunting-jacket joint),
but still I crawled in one red-and-white-checkered
pocket, through the womb of the lining,
and out the other (pocket), finding nothing
but a nuptial carrot, an aubergine –
say that slow: au-ber-gine –
and an old token that when examined
under the little microscope I received
on my eleventh birthday
would prove to allow passage
on a mode of transportation
long since extinct.
                    I'm a believer
in caution, my mamá taught me thrift,
but this carcassless jacket, this jacket
impersonating a furry tablecloth
in an Italian restaurant where I once dined
with a Greek professor who could quote,
to the word, the entire catalogue of the Swan

Silvertone Singers, would look good on my
back, keep me warm in these bitter
Canadian winters of yours
where even the dogs shiver
between games of pachisi.

WHAT WERE YOU *THINKING?*

I was thinking maybe I would like to have suction-cup fingers
and I could cling to your window at night
and watch all your silences.
I was thinking I would like classical music better
performed on a busy street
to the sounds of car horns and tossed pennies.
I was thinking how if instead of heads
people had parking meters
I could tell how much you liked me
by if you put in a nickel or a quarter
before twisting my nose.
What was I thinking?
I was thinking about a river of glass
smashing against the rocks on which I stood, about
being able to go deaf at will
and watch in silence,
slow down my eyes
and watch real slow,
become so small I'd be like a spore
and drift on the breeze
into a field of corn.

EMERGENCY

Her face
fluttered
low
over moist
blades
of grass and
past
an overturned
boll weevil.
A siren
wailed
in the forest.

THE MONUMENT

It is Sunday.
It is cold.
The son opens the door
and the father walks in slowly.
Goldberg sits in the back room
reading the sports page,
smoking an invisible cigarette.
Izenberg sits up front,
gazing into the papers
heaped on his tiny desk.
The shop is silent.
Goldberg and Izenberg are silent.
Monuments flank the father
and son – black, grey, white,
single, double, smooth, bevelled –
and the two walk up the aisle
like it's a wedding.
They look from Izenberg to Goldberg,
back to Izenberg, then to Goldberg.
The father places the two under shells,
shuffles them around,
pauses,
shuffles again, then lifts a shell.
It's Izenberg. Izenberg
made the stone for the father's

mother, and now he'll make one
for the father's wife. The father
wants a double, he's thought
long and hard, and he wants
a double. He asks which side
he'll lie on, and imagines the plot,
now covered with snow, and he turns
this way and that, till it finally
makes sense. They wander
among the headstones, father and son,
running their fingers
on the smooth and the rough,
across the letters
in Hebrew and English,
across the flowers, the stars,
the flames. The father remembers
his wife lighting candles
(had they once been devout?),
and he slumps in a chair
and closes his eyes. The son
flips through binders crammed with photos,
the monuments in action, and Izenberg
explains the fine points of each,
while Goldberg, in the back,
is on his third invisible cigarette.
Outside,
the huge willows bend,

a woman drops her keys in the snow,
a little Jewish dog
barks at a lamppost,
and the icebergs
begin to melt.

SEMPER FIDELIS

lichen clings
to my broken glasses

pelicans attempt
to determine
its species

i lie on my side
eyes wide
remembering the moment
of impact

in the sky's deep ink
a star blinks
then coughs

fidel castro
lights another cigar

GETTING TAUGHT

In bed he feels
the breeze of a centipede
in the next room.
He rings the little bell
and I pull up a chair,
lean close to his mouth.

I watch his chest rise and fall
and I know that
he knows
that in the sky
the clouds push the sun
off the edge of the canvas.
I feel that he
is my father, even though
he has never bowled. I
keep his words
in a chamber
beneath the ribs
that hug my heart. And
I hear him speak:

"Leave me.
My breath will find a way
to conjure a kiss

from the frozen ground.
Collect your children
and tie their hair together.
Gather them in your arms
and teach them my song.
I have a hunch
that flowers end
tomorrow. I give you
the sky; put it
somewhere safe."

He passes a withered hand
across his mouth
and his mouth is gone;
across his nose and eyes
and they're gone, too.
I feel a tickle at my feet
and see a river spilling
across the floor. My
shirt is warm now
on the sputtering rad.
Some light flows in
where the door
longs for the floor.

POP SONG

Imbecile,
you wait at the
train station
with your xylophone.
She will not be there
this time,
imbecile. That was
ten years ago.
Look at the date
on the newspaper.
Look at the headline:
She Leaves The Imbecile.
You are on a camel
galloping through mud.

ONE OF THOSE LAKES IN MINNESOTA

We're walking around again
slipping into evening
the insects biting
and we're circling just
one of the lakes in Minnesota
there's hundreds maybe
thousands and Debby's
trying to remember the name
of that sax player who plays
two maybe three instruments at once
and one with his nose and I think
Pharaoh Sanders Lester
Young Art Farmer who I
don't even know if he plays sax
but I used to think his name was
Ant Farmer but no
it's Roland Kirk Debby
remembers it's Roland Kirk she's
listening to these days
trying to learn to play
in spite of her
carpal tunnel syndrome
and speaking of car pools
her van that glorious monster
that brought her and Beth

and Becca and Charlie and
Michael (but not the Michael
who'll come up later in this
poem) to Toronto thru
Lansing Michigan what was it?
two years ago?
well that van
it's dead
just a huge flower-
pot behind her mom's house now
she tells me (that van
was a monster and it
brought these amazing people)
while behind us Michael
the other one
and Judy
are talking
heavy stuff like families
and politics
and Michael's voice is the
black surface of the lake glittering
beneath the stars under
Michael's favourite constellation
which I think is of some animal
a swan or
perhaps bill bissett
and Judy's voice is the smooth

shadows of birds darting
from tree to tree above us
and this lake is endless
tonight I mean we started walking
an hour ago and we're still going
and the insects are eating us
alive and that big lumpy shadow
ahead well it's a raccoon
and Debby's not crazy about
raccoons so we race by while
Michael and Judy stop to
watch and I'm telling you
this is just one of thousands
of lakes in this state but we
could spend a
wonderful life just walking
around this one over and
over again or just once
just one long walk that
takes us around for a life-
time and I say Rahsaan Roland
Kirk to show off I've heard
of him and Debby says yeah
and up by the road a
loud cluster of lights is
passing slowly it's
a motorcycle the

Macarena blaring from it
can you think of anything more
awful? but tonight
it's not awful
it's what makes
the lake
so beautiful
and my birthday passes
then another
then three of Judy's
six of Michael's
five of Debby's and
this is a big lake and a
long night and if
nothing else happens
in our lives
that's just fine
like Roland Kirk
playing perhaps
four instruments at once
one
with his nostrils

MISS ECUADOR

Down at the Latin festival, I saw Miss Ecuador take the
stage to lip-synch a couple of songs and profess her love
for Canada, although she pronounces it Canadá, with an
accent on the final "a", which is much prettier sounding
than Canada – the accent on the first syllable has an
almost dismissive air. But I'm being evasive. Here's the
thing: from where I was standing, Miss Ecuador, in her
clinging animal-print gown, looked eight feet tall. The guy
who introduced her, and the dancers who leapt about
behind her, they looked like midgets around Miss
Ecuador. This can only be explained one way: Miss
Ecuador hails from a small village on a mountain, whose
inhabitants, over the centuries, became accustomed to the
density of the air at that high altitude. Over the past
several decades, clearcutting on the mountain has caused
severe erosion, and as the mountain becomes shorter, the
people of Miss Ecuador's village become taller so they
can continue breathing the same air. And so Miss
Ecuador stands eight feet. A special plane had to be built
to fly her to Toronto for the Latin festival, at great
expense to the citizens of this city. But it was worth it,
just to have Miss Ecuador here, among us. Do not faint in
our rich, low-altitude air, Miss Ecuador. Do not be
overcome by the air of Canadá.

BILLIARDS AND POISON

All the channels say
there'll be a storm.
I'm no Muggins, about
to be stranded for
three days in a pool hall in León
while barrages of rain
pound the metal roof
and Samantha Fox and
Sly Stallone peel
from the yellowed walls, amid
the scrape of chalk against cue,
the din of
anxious laughter,
the yelps of emaciated
dogs, the clack
of the reds, the hiss
of the black.
Our table is the
deformed one in the corner,
chipped and torn, worn
down to its wooden surface.
I play with a warped cue,
and so does Dolores
and equally Joe.
The rain carries typhoid

through the gutters,

to the streets of the poor,

past the tanneries

where men stand knee-deep

in their own young deaths,

past shells of cars

with trees growing through them,

and children play in these streams.

They are famous actors

in Hollywood films

and nothing

frightens them.

LOOKING INTO MY ILLNESS

I was sitting in a sunlit, dusty restaurant
near the railroad tracks that sever
the capital of Guatemala. I had just seen
three quick kids roll a bony old man
in a market I'd been told to avoid
and now I felt like some soup
and a stack of salted tortillas.
These warnings, though:
I'd been warned against everything.
Do not befriend strangers on a train.
Do not fall asleep on the bus.
Do not photograph soldiers.
Do not give money to begging children.
Do not accept the first price given at the market.
Do not eat peeled fruit in the street.
Do not eat meat in the street.
Do not eat in the street.
Avoid political gatherings.
Do not ask locals about the violence.
Do not hike up the volcano alone.
Do not mention the FMLN, the FSLN, or the URNG.
Avoid tap water. Avoid ice.
And now I felt like a bowl of soup
and a stack of salted tortillas.
At a table beside me,

two men slept, snoring loudly.
At a larger table, four men laughed
and pushed at each other,
glanced at me and laughed some more.
A young student shared my table,
carefully printing the alphabet
on a sheet of lined paper.
I dipped a battered spoon
into a chipped bowl of cloudy soup.
I watched as strange grey lumps
rose to the surface and waved at me.
A fly walking the edge of the bowl
watched too.
The soup was warm and rich.
I ate it slowly,
pushing a piece of tortilla into my mouth
after every few sips.
Outside the restaurant,
a pickup truck screeched to a halt.
Two large men grabbed a youth from the road
and heaved him headfirst
into the back of the truck.
A man in uniform stomped on the boy,
then held on tight as the truck raced away.
I looked into the shallow puddle
that covered the bottom of my bowl.
Inside my belly

and through the winding tunnels of my intestines,

an idea was beginning to take shape.

A whole new way of being.

I was to have superdigestion.

I would sweat and ache,

and groan and curse.

I would blast my food from my bowels

almost before I'd eaten it.

HOW TO SUCCEED

RECREATING JIM

Jim falls into an open sewer in downtown
Managua. It is the rainy season. When he
emerges, his clothes are soaked, a page of
La Prensa is plastered to his leg, his cigarette
is doused, his back is wrecked forever. But
he is still Jim.

Jim dives into a vat of bubbling hatred. His
father emerges legless. His mother is too
nice, too nice, and he hasn't called her for
months. Soon his father dies. Jim soars from
the vat, still Jim, swoops low over Kingston
and howls. He wears a cape, which flutters in
the cool air. He is my hero.

Jim drives to Rattlesnake Point and climbs a
thirty-foot rock. He looks down and says,
"I've climbed a thirty-foot rock," smiles for
Jo-Ann's camera. He swings from side to side,
and bounces against the rock face, then comes
down, lights up a smoke, still Jim.

I am nine years Jim's junior but my hair is
greyer than his. I've fed his cats and cut
his grass and read his poems. Jim has put his

arm around my shoulders. He has taken from
his wallet a picture of his child and shown
it to me. It is his liver. He spins his liver
on his fingertip and talks about it for
hours. Jim is sober. His name is Roque
Dalton.

It is inevitable. Jim becomes a great black
epileptic dog, gnawing at my hands. He is an
animal healing itself, curled up in distant
warmth. Jim becomes a most frightening thing.
He becomes a man in a race against himself.
His fingers can't keep up with his
cigarettes. Jim becomes a bus, hurtling
north. He pulls a mask down over his face.
Jim is a telephone. He abandons his language
and learns a new one. Jim recreates Jim.

I can say nothing.

HOW TO SUCCEED

They are furtive, fluttery,

clustered around

the tiny

round table, leaning

into their beef dip,

whispering hoarsely

about their wives,

young girls,

kidney stones,

shuffling their

stockinged feet

under the chipped

glass table,

damp cigarettes hanging

from their lips,

while outside

prize-winning poodles

spin nearly

empty chambers,

put barrels

to fluffy ears,

pull triggers,

pant,

and repeat.

CONFINING SOMETHING PERFECT

after Mark Strand

Amid a glebe
I am the vacuum
of glebe.
This is
invariably the victim.
Wherever I happen
I am what is lost.

While I perambulate
I divorce the bubble
and invariably
the bubble budges
to gorge the void
where my carcass belonged.

We completely suffer from sanity
by budging.
I budge
to confine something perfect.

SURVIVAL

Wind blows cold through the palms
The lake is shattered by a thousand raindrops
Millions of microbes crawl over my body
The telephone rings in the next room

AFTER BLACKFLY SEASON

The birds are all facing
the wrong directions
like some avian
firing-squad joke

    *

July is the worm
that won't leave the earth
It cries, "Aroint thee!"
and clings to a segmented jesus

    *

The fireflies
compare abdomens
around the
weiner roast

    *

My head is thus –
a beautiful collision

SAY FWAY LUH LOOZ

I

Paintings fall off hooks, slide
down walls like
bullet-riddled gangsters,
leaving brown smudges.
The lights go out, man and woman
bump into furniture,
stumble, step
on lenses fallen
from jiggling eyeballs.

Some kind of noise?
I didn't hear no noise.

II

The sky becomes a slab
of wet cement, begins to fall,
everyone runs
in all directions, scattering
like blobs of mercury. It
gets real hot,
stuff starts exploding.
The cement lands, settles,
dries, hardens. Time passes,
hard to say how much.
White lines form
on the cement surface, cars begin
to arrive, stopping
in orderly rows, rows
that stretch as far
as the eye can see. But
there are no eyes. There are
only cars, and they behave,
they cause no trouble.

III

From somewhere in the tranquil
sea of cars, a faint tapping,
gradually louder, a scratching,
clawing, a metallic clunk,
the thud of a fist.
A cry from a trunk.

IV

It's real dark, so it's hard to say
what's lighting up that thing
rising on the horizon,
a great glowing rectangle,
over there, yonder, *allá*,
where the dark meets the dark.
There's a faint rumble,
the sensation of continents nudging,
of a tooth being pulled.
But there are no teeth.

The noise from the trunk
more frantic now, fists
pounding, feet thrashing,
a guttural howl.

V

The luminous rectangle
on the horizon,
the silver screen,
towers over the rows
of cars. Colours
on its surface
flicker so fast
you can't name them.
The light bounces
from the roofs of cars,
revealing a black sky,
with craters
where stars used to be.
This is the sky beneath the
sky, you can see its veins
and muscles. Actually, it's
pretty gross.

VI

Maybe ten minutes later, maybe
two hundred years, there's a
straining creak, a squeak.
A car trunk lifts and out climbs a kid,
stinking t-shirt, drenched jeans,
umbilical cord, baseball cap.
Hid in the trunk,
tried to sneak in, thought he'd
get in without paying, beat
the system, see the show for
free, *gratis*, no clams,
greenbacks, *centavos*.
What was he thinking? What
was this kid thinking?

LANDSCAPE

after Larry Fagin

The bright green apple sails over the white fence.
The small running shoe lies in an overgrown field.
The man rappels down the side of a skyscraper.
The happy mice burrow through the rotting garbage.
The Latvian hairdresser leaps with joy.
Malarial flies float dead in the gutter.
A paperboy takes a bow.

CIGARETTES

"I am a cigarette. I am a cigarette."

This is the unrelenting chant of the mob as it marches in step through the narrow streets.

"I am a cigarette. I am a cigarette."

No smoke climbs from the mob, and it has no filter.

"I am a cigarette. I am a cigarette."

Let us consider its words as a metaphor: Does the mob cause cancer? No, it is a mob. In a metaphorical sense, though, does the mob cause cancer? For example, would a local politician look out his or her window at the passing mob and say, "It's like a cancer." That, of course, would be a simile, but we are speaking metaphorically.

"I am a cigarette. I am a cigarette."

It is just a mob. It moves through the streets like a . . . like a snake! It appears on the local news broadcast that evening and its leader is interviewed. "I am a cigarette," she says. "I am a cigarette."

The next day the mob takes to the streets again.

"I am an epaulette. I am an epaulette."

Ah, we had heard wrong. We had heard wrong.

THE ONLY GOOD MOUSE

The toast leapt out of the toaster
and landed on my plate.
I'd only ever seen that
in cartoons.
A good omen, I thought,
for so crucial a day.
I smeared on the butter,
the jam, pulled
my coffee closer.
From the corner of my room,
I heard a little click –
the TV had turned itself on
for the morning news.
Unrest in Hong Kong,
300 dead in Peru,
tobacco companies
buying up hospitals,
another mutilated body
found in a laundromat.
The guy reading the news
was a cow
wearing a bow tie.
My eyes popped from their sockets
and snapped back in.
I reached for the remote,

tried to change the channel.
I saw then
that I was short a finger
on each hand
and I wore white gloves.
I yelped in horror,
my voice a piercing squeak.
The coffee mug fled
on tiny legs
and the toast begged for mercy.
I dashed from room
to room, my big round ears
slapping the door frames,
music following me everywhere.
I had a job interview at ten,
but I couldn't pry off
my little red shorts
or my big yellow shoes,
and the clock was laughing,
its hands spinning wildly
in opposite directions.
Down in the cellar,
I rummaged through drawers,
through trunks and cardboard boxes,
till I found what I needed.
The springs were rusty
but it would do the trick.

Back in the kitchen,
I got some cheese from the fridge,
and the eggs gasped in unison
as I broke off a chunk.
I set the trap in a likely place –
the floor beside the stove.
Then I stepped back,
lowered my little mouse snout,
and prepared for the mazes of heaven.

VERMIN

Outside it rained. He lay in bed. In the dark he felt calm, soothed. He listened for the click. Waited for the click. He knew he could wait forever. For the tiny door to fall shut. For the click of the door falling. A little plastic sound. And the whisper of a shuffling mouse. A mouse panicking. But he was calm and he could wait. He could wait all night, and the next, and the next. He could wait in his sleep. He was at peace. He breathed the dark. He listened like he breathed. A little click. A mouse in a box. Suddenly in a box.

IN THIS WORLD

In this world there were no insects. Or possibly there
were *only* insects. Sometimes I have difficulty
remembering details. Or perhaps it's a matter of
definition. Do we share a vocabulary? Are insects the
ones with six legs or the ones with two legs? Are they the
ones that walk on the ceiling or the ones that walk on the
floor?

And it gets worse. What are those ones that have four
legs? It's no piece of cake telling a story. No slice of pie.

Let me start again.

It was a warm, humid night and Bob was unable to sleep.
He had too much on his mind and he just couldn't shake
that which haunted him. Tired of tossing and turning, he
decided to take a walk, or possibly a flight. He got up and
walked across the floor, although it may have been the
ceiling, and –

I don't think this can really work. I feel somehow that I
do not have your complete confidence as narrator and the
crisis may be irreparable. Had I been less moral, or
perhaps more clever, I'd simply have chosen one path
and stuck to it. There would have been no questions and

probably the story would have been finished by now and we could all go get so drunk that we couldn't even stand on our own two legs. Or six legs. Or whatever.

FLIES

Could there be anything other than the large, spindly
spider perched on the ceiling of the shower stall? The
steam of the spray wrenches the bastard loose, and his
suspended waltz sends shivers through my spine, as if I
thought he could lower down and envelop me in the soft
chow mein of his spider embrace. And is there anything
else to fear, anything else to bother fearing? What about
the waves of liquid that rush through the street, three
metres high, again threatening to smother, always
smothering. To be washed away down the street, out of
the city, off the edge of the planet, and right the hell out
to the stars to drift into eternity, where finally I can rest, I
can think, I can catch my breath in that airless vacuum. A
vacuum that bangs against my door each morning, waking
me up, sending me tumbling amidst a tangle of blankets
to the floor, to smash away at the blameless alarm clock,
the alarm clock that isn't even wound.

Let me cry, then, let my tears finally reach my shoulders
from the floor, let me release that godawful flow of pain,
and scream so my voice echoes far beyond the confines of
my skull, heard maybe by that astronaut, yeah, that
astronaut, the one drifting without a lifeline further and
further away from the yolk of his life. I will no longer
have to beat the flies away from my head, no longer have

to beat into submission the rats that nip at my toes.

The most little puff of smoke rises from the top of my skull. Outside, the crowds are rejoicing.

PLAINTIVE POULTRY

As I told you earlier, I did not know where the terrible
wailing originated. I searched all the rooms, the closets
and cupboards, under and behind the various pieces of
furniture, and I found nothing. Yet I heard a plea like
that of the banshee emanating from every pore of my
home. My dog, unnerved more by my ill-disguised
agitation than by the wail, cowered beneath the kitchen
sink, oblivious to the dripping of the mouldy pipes above
his matted head. I knew that I would never be able to
sleep, and so I pulled on my overcoat and made for the
streets. And there, to my astonishment, I still heard the
cries, though louder now. The sound came from all
around, enveloped me like a sticky womb, so I could not
determine its source. Each street and alleyway I peered
down harboured the deafening terror. And yet none of my
neighbours were disturbed by it, judging at least from
their extinguished lights, and so I began to wonder if I
myself were actually haunted, as in the books I had read
so often as a child. Taken by a sudden and chilling panic,
I ran, ran as fast as my arthritic legs would carry me,
through the roads and lanes, between buildings, across
parking lots, until finally I dropped, exhausted, in the
middle of the children's playground. I lay on my back and
stared into the stars, the miserable howls of agony ringing
louder than ever in my skull. What dead relative was this,

what friend who had gone to the grave before I repaid a debt? I clutched the ground beneath me, and found an awful consistency bunching between my trembling fingers. The ground was neither hard nor muddy. It was strange and spiny, and yet soft and silken. I tugged hard and found myself looking at an enormous white feather, and at the same time, the plaintive cries came still louder, and I felt the earth itself shift. I rose closer to the stars, my face pressed against the sky, and then I began to move. The ride was rough and rapid, and as my eardrums cracked wide open, letting the howls fill my skull, it all became clear. Although I was gazing still into the moving sky, I saw before me a chicken. And I knew I had never seen anything before.

BURROWING

There I am, and
everything's so quick,
burrowing down, take a
deep breath, there's all
these metal strands
writhing past me as I go
deeper, deeper through
the soil, through roots
of weeds, that's right,
and those twines of thin
steel, like deathworms
wriggling in pools of
water on a grave.

I'm calling for help, for
the lifeguard, and I see
a screaming monkey in a
microwave oven, there's
nothing I can do, it's
out of my power, and I'm
sinking further down, and
the clay is caking in my
nostrils and ears, and
the bits of wire like so
many missiles are

drilling tunnels through
my flesh, covering me
with little red beads
wiped clean as I
slide through the hard
earth.

What's your phone number?
did I forget to call you?
there's a telephone booth
around here somewhere,
the hood of that car
is filled with
sticks of wood, you start
the motor and Boy Scouts
appear, I think there's
flowers at your door, the
least I could do, and as
the ground gets harder I
only fall faster, and I
wish I had a radio, I
wish I had some music.

How long will this last,
nobody clued me in, and
I'm feeling more sinewy
every minute, those wire

worms are cutting me to
ribbons, and I'm worried
I'll leave too large
a tip, should I have
worn my tuxedo for this?
it doesn't matter, but
thank god I didn't
because I have a potato
chip in this pocket and I
must learn to
ration it properly.

I feel like I'm being
studied, like there's a
one-way window and a
hundred students behind
it, taking notes, I'm
trying to smile but they
can sense it's false,
and I'm beginning
to hear music now, or is
that the blast of hydraulic
drills? it's really hard
to say, my ears are
filled with earth.

This is just like

dancing, which I was
never very good at, it's
like doing the alley cat,
except for the frequent
tiny stabs of pain, and
in the distance, I can
hear it like my own
heartbeat, children are
clashing the lids of
garbage cans, they're
going to war, they're
going to war.

ABOUT THE AUTHOR

STUART ROSS is the author of more than 30 poetry and fiction publications, including *The Inspiration Cha-Cha* (ECW Press) and *Henry Kafka and Other Stories* (The Mercury Press). A small-press activist for two decades, he is co-founder of the Toronto Small Press Fair, publisher of Proper Tales Press, and editor of *Mondo Hunkamooga: A Journal of Small Press Stuff*. A popular, provocative performer of his work, he has read widely in Canada, and narrowly in the U.S., the U.K., and Nicaragua. He is considering a name change to the ancestral Razovsky.